JSIS

Karen Liberatore

A PERSPECTIVES BOOK

ORDER DIRECTLY FROM
ANN ARBOR PUBLISHERS
P.O. BOX 1
BELFORD
NORTHUMBERLAND NE70 7JX

Series Editor: Penn Mullin
Cover Design: Francis Livingston
Illustrations: Herb Heidinger

International Standard Book Number: 0-87879-295-3

1 0 9 8
0 9 8 7 6 5

Contents

Chapter 1

The First Animal

Dead animals! Monster animals! Animals with two heads! Animals with no legs! This is what Oasis was facing, but . . .wait . . . let's start at the beginning with Jim and see how it all happened . . .

Jim Mack had lived in the small town of Oasis all his life. For nearly half of his life he'd been in charge of the town's water company. It wasn't a hard job, but it kept him busy. Jim had to make sure the pumps were always working. And they had to work right. If they didn't, the town wouldn't have water. Jim knew it wasn't exciting or dangerous work, but he knew his job was the most important one in town.

Oasis was right in the middle of a hot desert. No other towns were near it. It had been there for nearly 150 years because it had lots of water. It was the only place in the big desert where there was always water. It ran deep and cool in springs

1

under the ground. Without all that water, Oasis would dry up, and people would not be able to live there.

The pumps that Jim took care of got the water from under the ground. From there it went into two big tanks. One was green, and the other one was red. Jim used only one tank at a time. That way the other tank could fill up. Then he would use it and let the other one fill again. Pipes took the water from the tanks to all the homes, stores, and farms in Oasis.

There were high mountains all around the town. Dry, brown desert plants were everywhere. But in town the plants and trees were always green. Even so, the desert seemed to be saying, "Just run out of water, Oasis, and I'll dry you up like everything else around here."

Jim really liked his job, and he liked Oasis. About the only thing he didn't like was new people who came there. They usually wanted to change things. He still got mad when he thought about the people who had been at the old lab before it closed.

The United Chemical Company had built the lab in Oasis about thirty years ago. It wasn't right in Oasis. It was up on a small hill near the town. No one in Oasis really knew what was going on in the lab. No one really cared much either, except Jim. He didn't like the lab because it used so much water. But after a while the lab closed. No one in town knew why. The people left. And things got back to the way they used to be.

Now people from the state had told Jim he must put a chemical in the town's water. It was a chemical that every city and town was using these days. This is what the men had said. That meant Oasis had to have it, too. Jim didn't want to put anything in the water. He told those state men that the water in Oasis tasted fine. He tried to tell them that the water was safe and clean just the way it always had been. The men wouldn't listen. Instead, a month ago they had sent him some new pipes and a pump. They also sent him big jars filled with enough of the new chemical to last six months.

Jim had put the new pipes and pump on the green tank about two weeks ago. Just yesterday he had put the new chemical into that tank. The green tank was new. Jim had built it on the west side of the town. The red tank, on the east side of town, had been there for a long time. The town needed more water in the summer so Jim had built the green tank. This way, there would always be lots of water. The red tank would soon be empty.This is why he put the new pipes, pump, and chemical in the green one. He was almost ready to start using it, and later on a new pump and pipes for the red tank would be coming, too.

Jim could see the new green tank as he drove towards it. He also saw buzzards flying in a circle over the green tank. He hated them. Wherever there were buzzards, something was dying. Jim drove his truck up next to the tank. The buzzards were still flying over it. The noise of the truck didn't even scare them away.

"Those birds," he said, "I just don't like them at all." He waved his arms, but that didn't scare them away either. They just kept on flying around. They could smell something dying. They weren't going to leave until it died.

Jim walked around the tank. He looked at the new pipes. Everything looked fine. Then he looked back up at the buzzards and said, "Man, are we going to have a hot summer." He put his hand on the green tank he had built and said, "We're going to need you soon. People are getting thirstier now."

Jim took one more walk around the tank. Then he started back to his truck. That's when he heard a noise. It was terrible. He didn't know

Whenever there were buzzards, something was dying.

where it came from. He stopped and looked around. Then he heard it again. The buzzards didn't scare him but those sounds did.

It was quiet for a moment except for the wind and the buzzards. Then he heard that same sound for the third time. He thought it might be coming from under the tank. At first he was so scared, he thought he should go back to town.

Then he thought he should look under the tank. He ducked under a crossbeam and looked around. It was cool under the tank. And wet. Maybe there might be a small leak. Suddenly he heard that same sound again. It made him jump. He hit his head on one of the crossbeams.

"Ow! That hurt," he said. He started to rub the bump on his head. That's when he saw it. He stood there under the tank, so scared he couldn't move or talk. He had never seen anything so terrible in his life. The thing looked back at him. Then it moved. At first he couldn't do anything. Then he yelled and ran as fast as he could.

He got into his truck and drove down the road. Then he stopped. He sat there. Everything was quiet. He couldn't believe the terrible looking thing he had seen.

Under the green tank an animal lay dying. It was in some water that had leaked from the tank. Jim had never seen an animal like this before. It was terrible to think about. What could it be? Suddenly he knew. This thing, this animal, this monster had once been a nice, quiet little rabbit.

Chapter 2

More Animals

Timmy Lee Larsen was the son of the chief of police in Oasis. Timmy was the second person to find one of the animals that day. He was out near Old Man Swanson's windmill looking for lizards. He looked for them all the time. Once in a while he caught one. But most of the time they moved too fast. He was following one until he saw something else move. It was a snake, but he was used to snakes, so he wasn't scared.

Timmy was quiet. He walked slowly over to the snake. It was sitting on a big rock by the windmill. It didn't move. That's good, Timmy thought. Maybe he could catch it!

"Here, come here," he said quietly. He walked over to the rock. "Come to Timmy."

The snake moved its head to look at Timmy. Actually, the snake looked with *both* heads! Timmy was excited.

Oasis. We need to find out what is happening and why it's happening. Now let Jim say a few words."

Jim stood up and put his hands in his pockets. "Well," he said, "Well, we have some dead animals here."

"And a lot of desert, too. So what else is new?" said Tom Lamm, the town's best mechanic. People laughed and started to relax. They waited for Jim to say something else.

"Well," Jim said again, "I decided to call the state myself this afternoon. I was worried about the town's safety. Two state people are coming here in the morning. I just hope they know what they're doing this time."

"That's it!" said Tom Lamm.

"Yeah, let them work for their money," yelled the cowboy.

Jim smiled at the crowd. He liked it when people agreed.

The mechanic yelled, "Jim's sure got a lot to say for a man who talks to water all day."

Jim smiled. Then he yelled back, "Well, it's sure a lot more interesting to talk to than a bad carburetor."

Chapter 3

The Scientists and the Lab

Jim could see the car long before it got to town. It would take the state people another fifteen minutes to get to Oasis. That's how far away they were. The air was clean in the desert, but the car left a trail of dust behind it. That made it easy to watch.

Inside it were Paul Knight and Cassie Monroe. They were both scientists from the state health department.

"Finally here," Cassie said. She rolled down the window to let the morning air inside. "Sure is a small town. It's even hard to find on the map. I wonder how bad the problem is."

Paul drove the car slowly into town. Jim stood there waving his arms. "That must be Jim Mack. He's the guy who called," Paul said.

Jim started talking before they could even get out of the car.

"I figure you can use the old lab up on the hill. It's a science kind of place. It won't take long to fix up..."

"Wait a minute," Paul said. He put his hand on Jim's arm. "First, let's get some coffee and talk about this. We've been driving for hours. We're tired and could use some food."

Jim took Cassie and Paul to the Sunset Cafe for breakfast. Jim told them what had been happening. "All we were told," Cassie said, "was that animals were dying up here. They said you needed some help to figure out what was happening."

"It's not just that they're dying," Jim said. "It's the way they're dying."

"What do you mean?" Paul asked.

"We have found twelve dead animals. All of them looked terrible. They had huge heads or no heads. Same with the legs and the rest of their bodies," Jim said.

"We may have to stay here longer than we thought," Paul said. "You talked about an old lab. Can you take us there? We can probably work at that place."

Jim got in his truck. Paul and Cassie followed in the state car. The old lab was so near the town that it took only a few minutes to get there. Jim opened it up. Paul said, "Cassie, I think we can

work here. It looks like we may be here for a while. I'll get the things from the car." Paul went back to the state car. There were two big boxes filled with equipment they needed. Jim got one and Paul took the other.

Jim helped them open the boxes and take the things out. But first, Cassie and Paul had to do some cleaning. It was a mess. Then they were ready to figure out what was happening.

"Jim," Paul said, "can you tell us anything about the animals?"

"Well," Jim answered. "if it will help you, all the animals were found on the west side of town. I have Timmy Lee's snake and a rabbit in the car."

"Can you get those dead animals and bring them in to us?" Cassie asked. "We can start with them."

"Sure can," Jim answered. He went to his truck and came back with the two animals. He had put them in a bag.

Paul and Cassie both put on gloves. Paul took both dead animals out of the bag and laid them on the lab table.

"Jim, I think we have our first clue. Are you sure that all the animals were found on the west side of town? Could some have been found in other parts of the town?" Cassie asked.

"No," Jim answered. "Only on the west side."

"Jim," Paul said. "We are going to be very busy for a while. Can you come back later today? We may be able to tell you something by then."

"Fine. I have some things to do anyway. I'll see how things are in town. Maybe some more animals have been found," Jim said.

As Jim was leaving, Cassie called, "If you do get any more animals, be sure not to touch them. Put on gloves. Bring the animals back here to us."

Paul and Cassie started to work. They cut small pieces from the animals. They looked at these pieces through their microscopes. After three hours they were very tired, but now they knew something.

"Cassie," Paul said. "I think it is now clear that these animals died because something very strong got into their cells."

For another hour Paul and Cassie worked with the microscope. They did many more tests, trying to figure out what had gotten into the cells. There was something in the cells that just didn't seem right. What was it?

"Well, all we can do is keep on working," Cassie said. "Maybe we should call this informa-

They looked at these pieces through their microscopes.

tion into the main computer."

"That's a good idea. Let's give it a try. Maybe it will help," Paul said.

Cassie went out to the car radio to call in their problem. While she was outside Paul started to look around the old lab. He wondered what had been done there thirty years ago.

"I called the information into the main lab,"

Cassie said when she came back inside. "We have to call back in about a half an hour. They might know what has gotten into the cells. If they do, we'll be all set."

Paul was reading some old letters that had been left behind when the lab was closed.

"We should try to learn more about this lab, Cassie," he said. "Maybe it will help us."

"What do you mean?" Cassie asked.

"Well, they worked with chemicals here. There are so many man-made chemicals. We just don't know enough about them," Paul said.

Cassie wasn't too sure about this. "I know, Paul. But the old lab closed years ago. These animals are dying now. What does it have to do with the lab?"

Paul closed the desk drawer and stood up. "Maybe there's something here that we don't know about. Anyway, the state lab might come up with the answer. If it does, we can figure out why these animals are dying."

"I hope so, Paul. Whatever it is, it works fast and it's deadly. I hope that we find it soon. Before it finds someone from Oasis."

Chapter 4

Chlorine

Jim came by just after his lunch. He brought sandwiches and coffee for Paul and Cassie. They were still working when he walked in.

"I was so busy, I had forgotten I was hungry," Cassie said.

Paul looked up and saw the sandwiches and coffee. "Oh, that looks and smells good," he said.

They both stopped working and started to eat. "How are you doing?" Jim asked. He looked around at the microscopes and the other equipment Paul and Cassie were using.

"Jim, you were right. Oasis has a problem—a big one. Something has gotten into the cells of those animals. It is killing the cells. And as it does, it turns them into monsters," Cassie said.

"We don't know yet why this is happening. We're waiting to hear from the state lab. We have called them and told them everything we know," Paul said.

Jim looked at Paul and Cassie. He didn't say anything for a while. Then he asked, "How dangerous is it? Tell me straight. Are the people of Oasis safe?"

It was quiet in the room. Then Cassie answered, "No, Jim, they are not safe. This is a very dangerous thing."

"What should we do?" Jim asked.

"Give us one day — just 24 hours — before you tell anyone. If the people here get scared, you don't know what they may do. We want to know what's happening and why it's happening," Paul said.

Jim stood there thinking. "Well, I don't know," he finally said. "I sure would hate for something to happen to someone here in Oasis." He looked at Paul and Cassie and then said, "Nope, I can't do that. I have to tell these people something. They are my friends. They all know about the dead animals. I have to tell them something."

Again it was quiet in the old lab. Paul and Cassie looked at each other.

"OK," Cassie said, "you tell them whatever you feel is best. But give us a head start. We know this is a big problem. We think we can figure it out. But we don't want to scare anyone."

"You folks have never been to Oasis before, have you?" Jim asked.

"No," Cassie said, "we haven't. I don't even think we knew there was a town like this in the desert."

"I didn't think you'd heard of Oasis before. Not many people know we're here. We like it that way. This town is here because of the water that runs under the ground. It keeps us from drying up on this big desert. We can't let anything happen to that water — or to the town," Jim said. "I guess I like this town a lot. I don't like other people coming here to mess up things. I don't mean you. I mean like those state guys last month. Boy, that made me mad when they told me I had to put stuff in my water. They said every place uses it now."

"What was it?" Cassie asked.

"Chlor...chlor..." Jim tried to say the word.

"Was it chlorine?" Paul asked.

"That's it. Chlorine. Those people who worked in this here old lab used big words like that, too," Jim said. "We always laughed about those people. They always stayed by themselves. They never mixed with us in town. I didn't laugh long.

One day I saw them with big jars of stuff by the dry creek outside. They dumped a lot of whatever was in those jars out there. That was just before they left town."

Jim walked over to the window. He pointed to the dry creek bed. Then he said, "Look, you can see the green tank I built right over there. Sure looks pretty, doesn't it? It's just about ready to turn on, too. The red tank over on the east side of town is almost out of water."

Cassie and Paul didn't even hear Jim's last words. They were thinking about the old lab, the jars, and the creek.

"Did you say they dumped something from jars out into the dry creek bed?" Cassie asked.

"Yep," Jim said, "they sure did. Only the creek had water in it then."

Cassie looked at Paul. "We've got to find out what was in those jars. And quick!"

"Cassie, you and Jim look through the empty boxes and cases in here," said Paul. "I'll start in the next room."

"OK," answered Cassie. "Jim, why don't you start on that side of the room, and I'll take this side?"

Paul went into the next room while Jim and Cassie looked on shelves and in boxes.

"Tri-meena. That's what the jars say."

"Cassie and Jim, come here for a minute," Paul yelled. They both ran into the next room.

"Look at these," Paul said. He was standing in the middle of a room full of empty jars. Cassie was so excited she started to yell.

"Tri-meena. That's what the jars say. Tri-meena," she yelled. "All of them!"

"That's what it is all right," Paul said. He was

happy, and he was smiling. "Even though these jars are all empty, there might be something left in them. We'll test what we can find to make sure. But I'll bet it is tri-meena." Then he turned to Cassie and said, "Do you really think they dumped all of this outside in that dry creek?"

"I guess they could have. After all, remember, Paul, they used to think that tri-meena wouldn't hurt anyone," Cassie answered.

"Let's go out and test the ground around here," Paul said. Then he turned to Jim. "Show me right where they did the dumping, can you?" he asked.

"No problem," Jim said. "I couldn't forget that. It's almost right outside the back door."

Paul and Cassie ran to get some big bags. Then all three of them went outside.

"This creek used to run through Old Man Swanson's farm," Jim said. "Now it's all dried up."

Paul and Cassie started to get the soil from the old creek. They filled one of the bags.

"Let's test this bag first, right now. Then we'll get soil from other parts of the old creek," Cassie said.

They ran back into the lab. Paul started testing the soil. Cassie and Jim watched him as he worked. Cassie was writing down what Paul was saying and doing. Then he stopped.

"Cassie, we were right. There is tri-meena in this soil. And there's a lot of it," he said.

"I'll call the state lab and see what their computer says," Cassie called as she ran out to the car radio. When she came back in a few minutes later, she said, "Paul, they agree! This is tri-meena. For sure!"

"We just didn't recognize it," Paul said to Cassie. "Tri-meena is made from carbon. There is a lot of carbon in the world, Jim. Nature uses carbon in one way. Scientists use it in another way. We could tell that this was tri-meena from the way it was made. This is why we had to do so much testing. Most of the things scientists have made with carbon are used for killing insects."

Cassie looked at Jim. "That's why the plants haven't been killed. Tri-meena doesn't hurt plants. It was made to kill insects. Funny thing," she said, "tri-meena isn't used any more because it didn't even kill insects. It was too weak."

Jim looked at Paul and Cassie. "Now what?"

"First of all, don't let any one get around this lab and tell everyone to stay away from Old Man Swanson's farm," Paul said.

Jim told everyone he could. He told them to tell others. Then he made a lot of signs and put them all over town. The signs said: STAY OUT OF OLD MAN SWANSON'S FARM AND AWAY FROM THE OLD LAB. DANGER. DANGER. DANGER.

An hour later Jim met Cassie and Paul at the Sunset Cafe. Paul and Cassie were having a cup of coffee. "You sure got those signs up fast, Jim," Paul said.

"There hasn't been a dead animal all day. Maybe it's over," Jim said.

"Maybe," Cassie said. "At least we have a good start. Maybe that old creek was where all the dead animals had gone looking for water. Somehow they got the tri-meena into their bodies."

Jim looked out the window of the Sunset Cafe. "It's getting dark. I think I'll go home. We've had a busy day. See you in the morning."

"Good night, Jim. And thanks for all the help you gave us," Paul said. They shook hands and Jim left.

Paul and Cassie sat quietly after Jim left. They were thinking about the day and how hard it had been. They began to worry.

"Cassie, why do you really think tri-meena made those animals die?" Paul asked.

"I don't know, Paul. We saw tri-meena in the

animals and in the soil. But can tri-meena really do all that?"

Paul rested his head on the back of the chair. He was thinking. "Hmmm. I wonder."

Cassie jumped up from her chair. "The water! Paul, the water! We have to test it, too."

Paul jumped up, too. "That's right. We didn't even think of that. They dumped that stuff in the old creek. From the creek, it could have gone everywhere because the creek had water then!"

Cassie and Paul paid for the coffee and ran back to their car outside the Cafe.

Somewhere out of Oasis a little cow was lost and dying. It had no eyes. It was another monster!

Chapter 5

Fire in Town

Paul and Cassie saw lightning in the hills as they drove back to the old lab. They had hours of work to do that night. They had a new clue and they had to find out what it might mean.

"Looks like we're going to get some rain," Paul said as he was driving.

All of a sudden Paul heard the cry of the young cow. It was in the middle of the road. "Oh, no! Hold on, Cassie," Paul yelled. He stopped the car as fast as he could. The car turned and went to the right side of the road. Then it came to a stop.

"You OK?" Paul asked. Cassie held her arm. It hurt.

"It's nothing," she said. "What was wrong? Why did you stop so suddenly?"

"A young cow. We just missed it. It's right in the middle of the road. Let's see what's going on." They got out of the car.

"Is it dead?" Cassie asked. She looked at the body. It wasn't moving.

Paul turned on his flashlight. "It's not dead...yet. But it will be soon."

Paul and Cassie looked at the dying animal. They could see that the young cow had no eyes.

"Another one. And we thought there weren't going to be any more! We've got to get this animal back to the lab," Paul said.

Cassie ran to the car and got a blanket. They put the animal in it, took it to the car, and put it in the trunk. Then they started back to the old lab.

Just as they got there, it started to rain. There was lightning and lots of rain. They took the dead animal into the lab. By now it was raining very hard.

The first thing they did was to test wet sand from the old creek. It didn't take them long to find tri-meena in it. Everything they tested so far had tri-meena.

Paul and Cassie stopped. They didn't know what to do. Tri-meena couldn't hurt anything. And yet it was in everything they had tested.

"It has to be tri-meena," Paul said. "But I still don't feel sure about it."

27

"I've been thinking, Paul," Cassie said. "Maybe tri-meena by itself doesn't hurt anything. But maybe when it is with something else, it can hurt things."

"I think you may be right, Cassie," Paul said. "But what is it that we need to know?"

Cassie got up and walked over to the coffee pot. She turned to look out the window. "Hey, there's a fire in town. Looks like a big one."

Down in the town, everyone was trying to help. The old school was on fire. Lightning had hit it and started the fire. If it had still been raining, that would have helped. But the rain had stopped. Jim had to use water from the red tank to stop the fire. There wasn't much water left in it. But there was just enough to help stop the fire. The green tank, full of water, would have to be turned on sooner than Jim had planned.

Cassie and Paul watched the fire. When it was out, Paul said, "You know, Cassie, I grew up in a big city. I always thought a big city was the best place to live. But being here in Oasis, I don't know. It's so pretty. I would like to live in a place like this one of these days."

"So would I," Cassie said. "It just doesn't seem right that a place as pretty as Oasis should have all these things going wrong. Was Jim right? Do

The old school was on fire. Lightning had hit it.

people who come to Oasis hurt it? Look at that fire. We're here. Maybe we made it happen."

"Hold on there," Paul said. "Don't think like that. You're tired. We have worked hard all day. Remember, we're trying to help Oasis and the people."

"Help them?" Cassie said. "What have we done? What have we really done? Another animal is dead. Maybe others are dead. Ones we haven't found yet." She turned around and went to sit down. "I'm tired."

"Cassie, listen to me," Paul said. "That tri-meena was dumped here a long time ago. It was a bad thing to do but no one wanted to hurt Oasis. They didn't know tri-meena would do these things. Don't feel that way. I need your help."

"But why did it happen now and not then? Why did it happen all of a sudden?" she asked. Then she said, "Wait a minute. I have an idea."

Chapter 6

A New Lead

Paul looked at Cassie for a minute. She had a new idea. He hoped it was a good one. They still had to work fast to figure out what was happening in Oasis. If something was killing the animals in this town, it could kill people. They had to think of *everything* to figure this out. What if the people of Oasis started to turn into monsters? What a horrible thing to think! But maybe it could happen. They had to keep on working even if it meant 24 hours a day!

"Paul," Cassie said. She wasn't tired any more. She was ready to get back to work. "We haven't even thought about how the animals were killed. We just know that something got in their cells and killed them."

"Cassie, what are you trying to say?" Paul asked.

"Listen, Paul," she went on. "We know tri-meena got in the soil around the old creek bed. We know that the wind blew that soil around. We know that the only animals that have died were from this side of town. Animals have to eat. Most of them eat plants. Right?"

"That's right," Paul yelled. "If plants died, no one would think much about it. But when animals start to die, then people start asking about it!"

"We have to do two things, Paul," Cassie said. "We must find out if plants have been dying in Oasis. Then we must get plants and look at them under the microscope."

"Jim is the only one who would know about the plants," Paul said. "We have to find him."

"Bring the flashlights. We may need them," Paul called out as they ran to the car.

Paul and Cassie drove back into Oasis. The first place they went to was the Sunset Cafe. They thought Jim might stop there once the fire was out. He was there all right, talking with Joan.

Paul and Cassie got out of the car and ran into the Cafe. Jim was just getting ready to leave. "Jim, wait! Wait," Cassie called out.

"I was just going home," Jim said. "I'm tired from that fire. It almost burned the school down."

"Jim, we have another idea and we need your help again," Cassie said.

"OK, how can I help?" he asked.

"Come on with us. We don't have much time," Paul said.

The three of them went out and got into the car. "Jim," Paul said, "take us everywhere the dead animals were found."

"That's going to take some time," Jim said. "Can't we do it tomorrow?"

"Jim, we don't have a lot of time. We think the killer got into those dead animals from something they ate. We need to see the plants near where they were killed," Cassie said.

It took them three hours to drive to all the places. At each place Paul and Cassie pulled some plants from the ground. They went to Old Man Swanson's farm, to the green tank, and all over the west side of town. They filled the car with all kinds of plants and weeds. Cassie made sure that all the plants were not mixed up. She put each bunch in a different bag and marked each bag. Then they took Jim back to the Sunset Cafe to his car.

"I'm going home to bed," Jim called out.

"We'll be working all night if we have to," Cassie said.

Back at the old lab, Paul and Cassie got pieces of each plant. Paul took some and Cassie took some. They looked at the pieces through the microscopes.

At last they stopped. They were both tired.

"Paul, what did you find?" Cassie asked.

"Cassie, some of these cells look OK. Some look different. But none of them has been killed. There is tri-meena in all of them," Paul said.

"OK. Come here. Look at these cells. The plants came from the soil around the green tank," Cassie said.

Paul looked into her microscope. These cells were different. They had tri-meena, but something else was in those cells. Whatever it was, it was not the same thing they saw in the other plant cells.

"Paul," Cassie called, "get some cells from that cow we found. Put them under your microscope. I want you to see something."

Paul got the cells and a test tube. Then he set up the microscope.

Cassie took a look into it and said, "Paul, tell me what you see down there."

Paul looked through the microscope. He didn't say anything. He kept on looking. "I see the same things we saw before. Why? What do you think is there?"

"No, there's something else in those cells. They look like the cells from the plants from the green tank!"

"OK, Cassie. So what is it?"

"Chlorine."

"Chlorine? OK, I see the chlorine. But so what? Every town has chlorine. That's not a killer," Paul said.

"Every town but Oasis has chlorine," Cassie said.

"What?" Paul suddenly stopped. His eyes got big.

"Remember? Jim was talking about the lab. He said something about the state telling him to put chlorine in the water. He said the word chlorine sounded funny to him."

"That's right," Paul said, thinking back. "I do remember now. Oasis has never had chlorine in its water supply. How could we have missed that clue? Cassie, do you think that chlorine and tri-meena *together* kill the animals?"

"I think so," she said. "I think it does."

That's when it hit them! Jim had said that he put the chlorine into the green tank. And he was going to turn the green tank on as soon as the water in the red tank was used up.

"We've got to get to Jim before he switches the water supply to the green tank," said Cassie. "We don't want anyone in town drinking that water."

"You're right, Cassie," Paul said. "But it's too late now to see him. He's had a hard day, and I'm sure he's in bed. We'll get up early and go out to see him in the morning. He won't be turning on the water until then."

"I think I'll sleep better myself tonight," smiled Cassie.

Chapter 7

The Green Tank

Early in the morning, Paul and Cassie got into their car. They didn't even stop to have coffee. They needed to see Jim right away. They had to stop him before he turned on the green tank. As soon as the water from the green tank went into the pipes, it would go everywhere in Oasis. To the stores, to the homes—and to the farms. The farms grew all the food for Oasis.

Cassie didn't wait for Paul to stop the car at Jim's home. She jumped out while it was still moving. She ran up the stairs of Jim's home.

Moon, Jim's dog, started barking. "Be quiet. Nice dog, nice dog," Cassie said. Moon was sitting on the stairs. "Jim! Jim!" she called. And Moon kept right on barking.

Paul ran around to the back of the house and called Jim. Moon was right with Paul. He kept on barking. Paul kept on calling, "Jim! Jim! Are

"Jim! Jim!" she called. And Moon kept right on barking.
you there?"

"With all this barking and calling, I don't think
he is home. He would have come out by now,"
Cassie said.

"His truck's gone. I bet he's in town. Let's go,"
Paul said. Moon was still barking as they left.

Jim wasn't at the Cafe. Joan, the waitress, said
he'd been there and had left about ten minutes
ago.

"Hey," Joan called out, "did you hear about the fire last night? It sure was a big one. Almost burned the school down. Jim said this morning that we'd used almost all the water from the red tank!"

"That's it, that's it," Paul said. "Jim's at the tank!"

Cassie was talking to herself as Paul drove as fast as he could to the green tank. "Please, Jim, don't do it. Don't do it. Don't turn that green tank on."

Jim was there at the tank all right. Paul and Cassie could see him as they were driving toward the tank. Cassie started yelling before Paul stopped the car. "Jim, wait! Wait!"

Jim was looking at all the pipes. With just one little push, the water would start going through the pipes. Water would go every place in Oasis.

Paul and Cassie jumped out of the car and ran to Jim. "Jim! Jim! Wait!" Cassie called out. "Don't open the pipes. Wait!"

By that time Paul and Cassie were at the tank. Jim looked as if he didn't know what was happening.

"Jim! The water will end up killing everything in Oasis!" Paul said.

Jim looked at both of them.

"Did you? Did you open the pipes, Jim? Oh, please, I hope not," Cassie yelled.

Paul looked at Jim. "Is the water turned on, Jim?"

"I didn't turn on that water. I'll never turn on that water," he said. "I got to thinking about all of this last night. And when I got up this morning, I figured something out."

Paul and Cassie looked at each other. What was Jim trying to say?

Cassie sat down by the tank. She was tired but she wanted to hear Jim tell what stopped him from turning on the water.

"OK, Jim. Tell us why you didn't open up the water pipes," Paul said.

"Well, I'll tell you since you asked," Jim said. "That fire took a lot of water to put out. And it's been so hot lately, I figured I needed to start using the green tank. I went up to the red tank after the fire. Like I thought, it was just about empty. So I went home and figured I'd come up here this morning and give Oasis some new water today. But when I got home Moon started barking. He wouldn't stop. I went out to see why he was barking and you know what? That old dog was in a mud puddle. He's so old that when he went to drink some rain water from the puddle, he got

40

stuck in it. I laughed and laughed."

"Then what happened?" Paul asked.

"Anyway, that's when it came to me. I didn't even think about it until Moon was sitting in all that mud. I had seen a puddle last week when I went under this tank. That's when I first saw the rabbit that looked so terrible. So I figured I would see if that puddle was still here under the tank this morning. The puddle is still there. Water is still leaking out of the tank a little bit at a time."

Paul and Cassie didn't say anything. They wanted Jim to keep on talking.

"In the desert, all animals go where there is water. Even spiders go to the water. I saw a spider this morning under the tank. It's almost as big as a cat. I've never seen anything like it. I got sick just looking at it. And that's when I figured I wouldn't open the pipes. You two have some tests to do. Something is still wrong. I don't know what. But I know I shouldn't open the pipes."

It's a good thing you didn't," said Paul. "We think we know what the problem is."

"Fantastic!" Jim said. "Let me meet you at the Cafe in an hour and hear all about it."

"Great," said Paul. "We want to put in a call to state, and then we'll be ready for some coffee."

41

Chapter 8

Oasis

Paul and Cassie were having coffee at the Sunset Cafe. They were ready to go back to the city. They now knew that tri-meena and chlorine, together, could kill animals.

Jim came into the Cafe. "Can I have some coffee with you?" he asked Paul and Cassie.

"Sure you can," Paul said. "Come on and sit down with us."

"I just had a call from the state health department. They are coming to Oasis to clean up the dirt around the old lab. They want everyone to stay away from the lab and the green tank. And guess what? They are going to build a new tank for Oasis after they clean up the tri-meena around the lab," Jim said.

"Jim, when you built the green tank near the old lab, you didn't know about tri-meena being in the soil. The wind, over the years, blew soil over to where you built the green tank. It is sad that those animals died the way they did. But it is good that water was leaking out of your green tank. After you put the chlorine in the tank and that water leaked into the soil, it got into the plants that killed the animals and turned them into such monsters," Paul said.

"But what I can't figure out," Jim said, "is why I didn't want to turn on the water in the green tank. I don't know why I didn't want to do it but I just couldn't."

"Jim," Cassie said, "your feelings were right on! Our tests showed that the chlorine by itself in the water was OK. It was the chlorine and tri-meena together that was the killer for animals. We found something else, too. Our tests showed that chlorine and tri-meena don't kill plants, but they stay in the plants. When animals or people eat these plants, terrible things happen. That's why it's so great you didn't turn on the tank with the chlorine in it. If that water had mixed with the soil in which people grew their vegetables, I hate to think what might have happened. The people in Oasis have had a close call!"

"That's why, Jim," Paul said, "you had that feeling that it was not safe to turn on the water in the green tank."

"What about water now, Jim, that you can't use the green tank?" Cassie asked.

"Well, I've told everyone in Oasis not to use much water for a few weeks. That will give time for the red tank to slowly fill up again. We'll keep on using the red tank until the state builds a new one," Jim answered.

"You know, Paul," Cassie said. "I really do like the water here in Oasis. It's good."

"Well, you know," Paul said, "I was hoping that Jim would give us a jar of it to take back to the city. Will you, Jim?"

"I think I can do that," Jim answered.

Jim got two jars and filled them with water. He gave one to Paul and one to Cassie. "You know," he said. "I guess other people coming into Oasis isn't so bad after all."

Paul and Cassie got into the car. Jim and Joan waved.

Paul and Cassie drove off. They looked at one another. They knew they'd be back soon.